# Fall Is Not Easy

written & illustrated
by
Marty Kelley

Zino Press
CHILDREN'S BOOKS
Madison, WI

This book is for my family
and my art critic wife, Kerri.
She just knows...

Thanks to Carolyn for the idea.

**Fall Is Not Easy** is published by Zino Press Children's Books, PO Box 52, Madison, Wisconsin, 53701. Contents copyright © 1998 by Marty Kelley. All rights reserved. No parts of this book may be reproduced in any way, except for brief excerpts for review purposes, without the express written permission of Zino Press Children's Books. Printed in U.S.A.

Written and illustrated by Marty Kelley. Art direction by Patrick Ready.

Kelley, Marty.
    Fall is not easy / written and illustrated by Marty Kelley.
       p.   cm.
    Summary: A tree tells why, out of all four seasons, autumn is the hardest.
    ISBN 1-55933-234-4
    [1. Seasons —Fiction. 2. Trees—Fiction. 3. Stories in rhyme.]
  I. Title.
  PZ8.3.K298Fal 1998
  [E] —dc21                         98-22574
                                        CIP
                                        AC

10 9 8 7 6 5 4 3 2 1
First Printing, September 1998

Fall
Is
Not
Easy

Winter is easy.

My branches are bare.

Then snow starts to melt

And spring's in the air.

Springtime is easy.

Green leaves start to grow.

Then spring rains are followed

By the summer sun's glow.

Summer is easy.

Just bask in the sun.

Then breezes blow cooler

And summer is done.

Fall is not easy.

It's time for a change.

Green leaves turn colors,

But mine all look strange.

That isn't right.

And that's just all wrong.

My colors won't go

Where I think they belong.

My leaves should be fire,

All brilliant and bright.

And I try and I try,

But they won't come out right.

And just when my patience

Begins to wear thin,

My leaves all fall off

And winter blows in.

Winter is easy.